SAN FRANCISCO BLUES

BY JACK KEROUAC

The Town and the City
On the Road
The Subterraneans
The Dharma Bums
Doctor Sax
Maggie Cassidy
Mexico City Blues
Visions of Cody
The Scripture of the Golden Eternity
Tristessa
Lonesome Traveler
Book of Dreams
Pull My Daisy
Big Sur
Visions of Gerard
Desolation Angels
Satori In Paris
Vanity of Duluoz
Scattered Poems
Pic
Pomes All Sizes
Heaven and Other Poems
Old Angel Midnight
Good Blonde & Others
The Portable Jack Kerouac
Selected Letters: 1940–1956
Book of Blues

JACK KEROUAC

SAN FRANCISCO BLUES

penguin books

PENGUIN BOOKS

Published by the Penguin Group
Penguin Books USA Inc., 375 Hudson Street,
New York, New York 10014, U.S.A.
Penguin Books Ltd, 27 Wrights Lane,
London W8 5TZ, England
Penguin Books Australia Ltd, Ringwood,
Victoria, Australia
Penguin Books Canada Ltd, 10 Alcorn Avenue,
Toronto, Ontario, Canada M4V 3B2
Penguin Books (N.Z.) Ltd, 182–190 Wairau Road,
Auckland 10, New Zealand

Penguin Books Ltd, Registered Offices:
Harmondsworth, Middlesex, England

Published in Penguin Books 1995

"San Francisco Blues" is one of the eight poems in Jack Kerouac's
Book of Blues, published by Penguin Books.

ISBN 0 14 60.0118 4

Printed in the United States of America

San Francisco Blues was my first book of poems, written back in 1954 & hinting the approach of the final blues poetry form I developed for the *Mexico City Blues*.

In my system, the form of blues choruses is limited by the small page of the breastpocket notebook in which they are written, like the form of a set number of bars in a jazz blues chorus, and so sometimes the word-meaning can carry from one chorus into another, or not, just like the phrase-meaning can carry harmonically from one chorus to the other, or not, in jazz, so that, in these blues as in jazz, the form is determined by time, and by the musician's spontaneous phrasing & harmonizing with the beat of the time as it waves & waves on by in measured choruses.

It's all gotta be non stop ad libbing within each chorus, or the gig is shot.

—Jack Kerouac

SAN FRANCISCO BLUES

1ST CHORUS

I see the backs
Of old Men rolling
Slowly into black
Stores.

2ND CHORUS

Line faced mustached
Black men with turned back
Army weathered brownhats
Stomp on by with bags
Of burlap & rue
Talking to secret
Companions with long hair
In the sidewalk
On 3rd Street
San Francisco
With the rain of exhaust
  Plicking in the mist
  You see in black
  Store doors—
  Petting trucks farting—
  Vastly city.

3RD CHORUS

3rd St Market to Lease
Has a washed down tile
Tile entrance once white
  Now caked with gum
Of a thousand hundred feet
Feet of passers who
  Did not go straight on
Bending to flap the time
Pap page on back
With smoke emanating
From their noses
But slowly like old
  Lantern jawed junkmen
  Hurrying with the lump
  Wondrous potato bag
    To the avenues of sunshine
    Came, bending to spit,
  & Shuffled awhile there.

4TH CHORUS

The rooftop of the beatup
   tenement
      On 3rd & Harrison
      Has Belfast painted
      Black on yellow
        On the side
      the old Frisco wood is
      shown with weatherbeaten
rainboards & a
washed out blue bottle
once painted for wild
      commercial reasons by
      an excited seltzerite
        as firemen came last
afternoon & raised the
ladder to a fruitless
      fire that was not there,
      so, is Belfast singin
        in this time

5TH CHORUS

when brand's forgotten
   taste washed in
   rain the gullies broadened
   & every body gone
the acrobats of the
   tenement
      who dug bel fast
      divers all
   and the drivers all dove

ah
   little girls make
   shadows on the
   sidewalk shorter
than the shadow
   of death
      in this town—

6TH CHORUS

Fat girls
In red coats
With flap white out shoes

   Monstrous soldiers
   Stalk at dawn
Looking for whores
   And burning to eat up

Harried Mexican Laborers
   Become respectable
   In San Francisco
Carrying newspapers
Of culture burden
And packages of need
Walk sadly reluctant
   To work in dawn
Stalking with not cat
In the feel of their stride
   Touching to hide the sidewalk,
   Blackshiny lastnight parlor
   Shoes hitting the slippery
With hard slicky heels
   To slide & Fall:
      Breboac! Karrak!

7TH CHORUS

Dumb kids with thick lips
And black skin
Carry paper bags
Meaninglessly:
"Stop bothering the cat!"
His mother yelled at him
Yesterday and now
He goes to work
Down Third Street
In the milky dawn
Piano rolling over the hill
To the tune of the English
Fifers in some whiter mine,
'Brick a brack,
Pliers on your back;
Mick mack
Kidneys in your back;
   Bald Boo!
Oranges and you!
   Lick lock
   The redfaced cock'

8TH CHORUS

Oi yal!
She yawns to lall
  La la—
  Me Loom—
      The weary gray hat
      Peacoat ex sailor
      Marining meekly
      Hands a poop a pocket
      Face
      Lips
Oh   Mo   Sea!
  The long fat yellow
  Eternity cream
  Of the Third St Bus
  Roof swimming like
  A monosyllable
  Armored Mososaur
  Swimming in my Primordial
  Windowpane
      Of pain

9TH CHORUS

Alas! Youth is worried,
Pa's astray.
What so say
  To well dressed ambassadors
  From death's truth
  Pimplike, rich,
  In the morning slick;
  Or sad white caps
  Of snowy sea men
  In San Francisco
Gray streets
  Arm waving to walk
  The Harrison cross
    And earn later sunset
    purple

10TH CHORUS

Dig the sad old bum
No money
Presuming to hit the store
And buy his cube of oleo
For 8 cents
So in cheap rooms
At A M 3 30
He can cough & groan
In a white tile sink
By his bed
Which is used
To run water in
And stagger to
In the reel of wake up
Middle of the night
Flophouse Nightmares—
His death no blackern
Mine, his Toast's
Just as well buttered
And on the one side.

11TH CHORUS

There's no telling
What's on the mind
Of the bony
    Character in plaid
Workcoat & glasses
    Carrying lunch
    Stalking & bouncing
        Slowly to his job

Or the beauteous Indian
Girl hurrying stately
    Into Marathon Grocery
Run by Greeks
    To buy bananas
        For her love night,
What's she thinking?
    Her lips are like cherries,
Her cheeks just purse them out
All the more to kiss them
And suck their juices out.

12TH CHORUS

A young woman flees an old man,
Mohammedan Prophecy:
And she got avocados
Anyhow.

   The furtive whore
   Looks over her shoulder
While unlocking the door
   Of the tenement
   Of her pimp
Who with big Negro Arkansas
Or East Texas Oilfields
Harry Truman hat's
   Been standin on the street
      All day
      Waiting for the cold girl
      Bending in thincoat in the wind
      And Sunday afternoon drizzle
      To step on it & get some bread
         For Papa's gotta sleep tonite
         And the Chinaman's coming back

13TH CHORUS

"No hunger & no wittles
neither dreary"
Said the crone
To Edwin Drood

Okay.
There'll be an answer.
Forthcoming
When the morning wind
Ceases shaking
The man's collar
When there's no starch in't
And Acme Beer
Runs flowing
Into dry gray hats.
When
Dearie
The pennies in the
palm multiply
as you watch

14TH CHORUS

When whistlers stop scowling
Smokers stop sighing
Watchers stop looking
And women stop walking

When gray beards
Grow no more
And pain dont
Take you by surprise
    And bedposts creak
    In rhythm not at morn
    And dry men's bones
    Are not pushed
    By angry meaning pelvic
        Propelled legs of reason
        To a place you hate,
        Then I'll go lay my crown
Body on the heads of 3 men
    Hurrying & laughing
        In the wrong direction,
                my Idol

15TH CHORUS

Sex is an automaton
Sounding like a machine
Thru the stopped up keyhole
—Young men go fastern
  Old men
  Old men are passionately
    breathless
Young men breathe inwardly
Young women & old women
Wait

There was a sound of slapping
When the angel stole come
And the angel that had lost
  Lay back satisfied

Hungry addled red face
With tight clutch
  Traditional Time
  Brief case in his paw
Prowls placking the pavement
  To his office girl's
    Rumped skirt at 5's
      Five O Clock Shadows

16TH CHORUS

Angrily I must insist—
The phoney Negro
Sea captain
With the battered coat
Who looks like
Charley Chaplin in a
movie about now filmed
   in the air by crews
   of raving rabid
   angels drooling happi
ly
      among the funny fat
      Cherubim
Leading that serious
   Hardjawed sincere
   Negro stud
In at morn
      For a round of crimes
      Is Lucifer the Fraud

17TH CHORUS

Little girls worry too much
For no one will hurt them
Except the beast
Whom they'd knife
In another life
In the as well East
As West of Bethlehem
And do of it much

  Rhetorical Third Street
Grasping at racket
   Groans & stinky
     I've no time
     To dally hassel
     In your heart's house,
     It's too gray
     I'm too cold—
     I wanta go to Golden,
       That's my home.

18TH CHORUS

I came a wearyin
From eastern hills;
Yonder Nabathacaque recessit
The eastward to Aurora rolls,
Somewhere West of Idalia
Or east of Klamath Falls,
One—Lost a blackhaired
    Woman with thin feet
    And red bag hangin
    Who usta walk
      Down Arapahoe Street
    In Denver
      And made all the
        cabbies cry
    And drugstore ponies
    Eating pool in Remsac's
    Sob, to See so Lovely
    All the Time
      And all so Tight
      And young.

19TH CHORUS

Pshaw! Paw's Ford
Got Lost in the Depression
He driv over the Divide
   And forgot to cleave the road
Instead put atomic energy
In the ass of his machine
And flew to find
   The gory clouds
Of rocky torment
   Far away
   And they fished him
   Outa Miner's Creek
   More dead n Henry
   And a whole lot fonder,
Podner—
     Clack of the wheel's
     My freight train blues

Third Street I seed

20TH CHORUS

And knowed
  And under ramps I writ
  The poems of the punk
  Who met the Fagin
    Who told him 'Punk
  When walkin with me
    To roll a Sleepin drunk
  Dont wish ya was back
    Home in yr mother's parlor
    And when the cops
      Come ablastin
  With loaded 45's
    Dont ask for gold
  Or silver from my purse,
    Its milken hassel
    Will be strewn
      And scattered
      In the sand
      By an old bean can
        And dried up kegs
          We'd a sat & jawed on—

21ST CHORUS

Roll my bones
In the Mortiary
　　My terms
　　　And deeds of mortgagry
　　And death & taxes
　　　All wrapt up.'

Little anger Japan
　　Strides holding bombs
To blow the West
　　To Fuyukama's
Shrouded Mountain Top
　　So the Lotus Bubble
Blossoms in Buddha's
　　Temple Dharma Eye
May unfold from
　　　Pacific Center
　　　Inward Out & Over
　　　　The Essence Center World

22ND CHORUS

For the world's an Eye
And the universe is Seeing
Liquid
Rare
Radiant.

Eccentrics from out of town
   Better not fill in
      This blank
   For a job on my gray boat
   And Monkeysuits I furnish.

   Batteries of ad men
   Marching arm in arm
      Thru the pages
      Of Time & Life

23RD CHORUS

The halls of M C A

Singing Deans
In the college morning
Preferable to dry cereal
When no corn mush

Cops & triggers
Magazine pricks
   Dastardly Shadows
And Phantom Hero ines.

Swing yr umbrella
   At the sidewalk
   As you pass
   Or tap a boy
      On the shoulder
      Saying "I say
      Where is Threadneedle
                        Street?"

24TH CHORUS

San Francisco is too sad
Time, I cant understand
Fog, shrouds the hills in
Makes unshod feet so cold
Fills black rooms with day
  Dayblack in the white windows
  And gloom in the pain of pianos:
Shadows in the jazz age
  Filing by; ladders of flappers
  Painters' white bucket
  Funny 3 Stooge Comedies
    And fuzzy headed Hero
    Moofle Lip suckt it all up
    And wondered why
    The mild & cream of heaven
      Was writ in gold leaf
      On a book—big eyes
      For the world
        The better to see—

25TH CHORUS

And big lips for the word
And Buddhahood
And death.
  Touch the cup to these sad lips
Let the purple grape foam
In my gullet deep
  Spread saccharine
    And crimson carnadine
    In my vine of veins
  And shoot power
    To my hand
      Belly heart & head—
        This Magic Carpet
        Arabian World
        Will take us
          Easeful Zinging
        Cross the Sky
        Singing Madrigals

26TH CHORUS

To horizons of golden
Moment emptiness
Whither whence uncaring
    Dizzy ride in space
        To red fires
        Beyond the pale,
        Rosy gory outlooks
        Everywhere.

San Francisco is too old
    Her chimnies lean
        And look sooty
    After all this time
        Of waiting for something
        To happen
        Betwixt hill & house—
        Heart & heaven.

27TH CHORUS

San Francisco
San Francisco
You're a muttering bum
   In a brown beat suit
   Cant make a woman
   On a rainy corner

Your corners open out
San Francisco
To arc racks
Of the Seals
   Lost in vapors
   Cold and bleak.

28TH CHORUS

You're as useless
As a soda truck
Parked in the rain
With cases of pretty red
   Orange green & Coca Cola
     Brown receiving rain
   Drops like the sea
     Receiveth driving spikes
Welling in the navel void.

I also have loud poems:
Broken plastic coverlets
   Flapping in the rain
     To cover newspapers
     All printed up
       And plain.

29TH CHORUS

Guys with big pockets
In heavy topcoats
   And slit scar
   Head bands down
   The middle of their hair
   All Bruce Barton combed
      Stand surveying Harrison
      Folsom & the Ramp
         And the redbrick clock
      Wishin they had a woman
      Or some money, honey

Westinghouse Elevators
Are full of pretty girls
With classy cans
   And cute pans
   And long slim legs
   And eyes for the boss
   At quarter of four.

30TH CHORUS

Old Age is an Indian
With gray hair
And a cane
In an old coat
  Tapping along
  The rainy street
    To see the pretty oranges
  And the stores
    On his big day
When the dog's let out.

Somewhere in this snow
I see little children raped
By maniacal sex fiends
Eager to make a break
But the F B I
In the form of Ted
  Stands waiting
    Hand on gun
  In the Paranoiac
    Summer time
    To come.

31ST CHORUS

I knew an angel
  In Mexico City
Call'd La Negra
Who the Same eyes
    Had as Sebastian
    And was reincarnated
      To suffer in the poker
      House rain
      Who had the same eyes
        As Sebastian
      When his Nirvana came

Sambati was his name.

Must have had one leg once
And expensive armpit canes
    And traveled in this rain
    With youthful hidden pain

32ND CHORUS

Beautiful girls
  Just primp
    But beautiful boys
    Do suffer.

White wash rain stain
Gravel roof glass black
  Red wood blue neon
  Green elevators
  Birds that change color
  And white ants
    Climbing to your knee
    Earnest for deliverance.

33RD CHORUS

It was a mournful day
The B O Bay was gray
Old man angry-necks
Stomped to escape sex
And find his Television
In the uptown vision
    Of the milk & secret
        Blossom curtain
        Creak it.

Cheese it the cops!
Ram down the lamb!
    700 Camels
    In Pakistan!

Milk will curdle, honey,
If you sit on stony penises
Three times moving up & down
And 7 times around

34TH CHORUS

While young boys peek
  In the Hindu temple window
    To grow
      And come
    To A-mer-ri-kay
      And be long silent types
      In the night clerk cage
    Waiting for railroad calls
      And hints from Pakistan
      Beluchistan and Mien Mo
      That Mahatmas
      Havent left the field
        And tinkle bells
        And cobra flutes
        Still haunt our campfires
      In the calm & peaceful
        Night—
          Stars of India

35TH CHORUS

And speak bashfully
  Thru strong brown eyes
  Of olden strengths
    And bad boy episodes
    And a father
      With sacred cows
    A wandering in his field.
    "Rain on, O cloud!"

  The taste of worms
  Is soft & salty
  Like the sea,
  Or tears.

  And raindrops
  That dont know
You've been deceived
Slide on iron
  Raggedly gloomy

36TH CHORUS

Falling off in wind.

I got the San Francisco
   blues
Bluer than misery
I got the San Francisco blues
Bluer than Eternity
     I gotta go on home
     Fine me
     Another
     Sanity

  I got the San Francisco
    blues
Bluer than heaven's gate,
    mate,
  I got the San Francisco blues
Bluer than blue paint,
    Saint,—
      I better move on home
      Sleep in
        My golden
        Dream again

37TH CHORUS

I got the San Acisca blues
Singin in the street all day
    I got
    The San Acisca
    Blues
Wailin in the street all day
    I better move on, podner,
    Make my West
    The Eastern Way—

San
  Fran
Cis
  Co—
San
  Fran
Cis
  Co
    Oh—
      ba
        by

38TH CHORUS

Ever see a tired
    ba by
Cryin to sleep
    in its mother's arms
Wailin all night long
    while the locomotive
Wails on back
A cry for a cry
In the smoke and the lamp
Of the hard ass night

  That's how I
    fee-
      eel—
  That's how
    I fee-eel!
That's *how*
    I feel—
What a deal!
Yes I'm goin ho
        o
          ome

39TH CHORUS

Yes I'm goin
> on
>> home
>>> today

Tonight I'll be ridin
The 80 mile Zipper
And flyin down the Coast
Wrapt in a blanket

Cryin
And cold

So brother
Pour me a drink
> I got lots of friends
> From coast to coast
> And ocean to ocean
>> girls
>> But when I see
>> A bottle a wine
>> And see that it's full
>> I like to open it
>>> And take of it my fill

40TH CHORUS

And when my head gets dizzy
And friends all laugh
And money pours
    from my pocket
And gold from my ears
And silver flies out
    and rubies explode
I'll up & eat
And sing another song
And drop another grape
  In my belly down

Cause you know
What Omar Khayyam said
  Better be happy
  With the happy grape
  As make long faces
    And groan all night
      In search of fruit
        That dont exist

41ST CHORUS

So Mister Engineer
And Mister Hoghead
    Conductor Jones
And you head brakeman
    And you, tagman
            on this run
    Give me a hiball
Boomer's or any kind
    Start that Diesel
    All 3 Units
        Less roll on down that rail
        See Kansas City by dawn
        Or grass of Amarilla
Or rooftops of Old New York
    Or banksides green with grass
            In April
                Anywhere

42ND CHORUS

I'd better be a poet
Or lay down dead.

Little boys are angels
Crying in the street
Wear funny hats
Wait for green lights
  Carry bust our tubes
    Around their necks
    And roam the railyards
    Of the great cities
      Looking for locomotives
    Full of shit
      Run down to the waterfront
      And dream of Cathay
      Hook spars with Gulls
        Of athavoid thought.

43RD CHORUS

Little Cody Deaver
A San Francisco boy
   Hung by hair of heroes
Growing green & thin
   And soft as sin
   From the tie piles
Of the railer road
   Track where Tokay
   Bottles rust in dust
   Waiting for the term
   Of partiality
   To end up there
     In heaven high
     So's loco can
     Come home
     Con poco coco.

44TH CHORUS

Little heroes of the dead
Found a nickle instead
And bought a Borden half & half
   Orange Sherbert & vanil milk
     Trod the pavements
     Of unfall Frisco
     Waiting for its earthquake
   To waver houses men
     And streets to spindle
     Drift to fall at Third
     Street Number 6–15
   Where Bank now stands
Jack London was born
And saw gray rigging
At the 'barcadero
   Pier, His bier
   commemorated in marble
   To advertise the stone
     Of vaults where money rots.

45TH CHORUS

Inquisitive plaidshirt
Pops look at trucks
In the afternoon
While Mulligan's
Stewing on the stove
And Calico spreads
   Her milk & creamy legs
   For advertising salesman
     Passing thru from Largo
   Oregon where water
     Runs the Willamette down
     By blasted to-the-North
       Volcanic ashes seft.

46TH CHORUS

Babies born screaming
    in this town
Are miserable examples
    of what happens
Everywhere.

   Bein Crazy is
   The least of my worries.

Now the sun's goin down
In old San Fran
   The hills are in a haze
   Of Shroudy afternoon—
Bent withered Burroughsian
Greeks pass
   In gray felt hats
   Expensively pearly
   On bony suffer heads

47TH CHORUS

And old Indian bo's
With no stockings on
  Just Chinese Shuffle
  Opium shoes
Take the snaily constitutional
  Down 3rd St gray & lost
  & Hard to see.

Tragic Burpers
With scars of snow
Bound bigly
Huge to find it
To the train
  Of time & pain
Waiting at the terminal.

Young punk mankind
  Three abreast
    Go thriving downwards
      In the hellish street.

48TH CHORUS

Red shoes of the limpin whore
Who drags her blues
  From shore to shore
    Along the stores
    Lookin for a millioinaire
      For her time's up
      And she got no guts
      And the man aint comin
      And I'm no where.

He aint done nothin
  But change hats
And go to work
And light a new cigar
  And stands in doorway
Swingin the 8 inch
Stogie all around
  Arc ing to see
Mankind's vast

49TH CHORUS

Sea restless crown
Come rolling bit by bit
  From offices of gloom
  To homes of mortuary
  Hidden Television
  Behind the horse's
    Clock in Hopalong
    The Burper's bestfriend
      Ten gat waving
      Far from children
      Sadly waving
      From the balcony
      Above this street
    Where Acme Paper
        Torn & Tattered
S'down the parade
Thrown to celebrate
McParity's return:

50TH CHORUS

All ties in
Like anacin.

Well
    So unlock the door
    And go to supper
And let the women cook it,
    Light's on the hill
    The guitar's a-started
        Playing by itself
        The shower of heaven notes
        Plucked by a gypsy woman
        In some old dream
            Will bless it all
                I see furling out
                Below—

51ST CHORUS

The laundress has bangs
  And pursy lips
  And thin hips
  And sexy walk
And goes much faster
 When she knows
  The booty in her
   laundry bag
  Is undiscovered
   And unknown
  And so no cops watching
    she steps on it
    t'escape the Feds
    of Wannadelancipit
    Here in the Standard
      Building
    Flying High
     the
    Riding Horse
   A Red—

52ND CHORUS

None of this means
anything
   For krissakes speak up
        & be true
     Or shut up
     & Go to bed

Dead

      The wash is waving goodbye
      Towards Oakland's russet

I know there are huge clouds
Ballooning beyond the bay

      And out Potato Patch,
      The snowy sea away,
      The milk is furling
        Huge and roly
          Poly burly puffy

53RD CHORUS

Pulsing push
To come on in
Inundate Frisco
  Fill the rills
And ride the ravines
And sneak on in
With Whippoorwill
    To-hoo—To-wa!
      The Chinese call it woo
      The French les brumes
      The British
        Fog
L A
    Smog
Heaven
    Cellar door

54TH CHORUS

Communities of houses
Caparisoned by sunlight
On the last & fading hill
Of America a-rollin
  Rollin
To the Western Chill

And delicacies of statues
Hewn by working men
Neoned, tacked on,
Pressed against the sign
  Mincin
  Mincin
To see the swellest coupon

Understand?

Light on the fronts
  of old buildings
Like in New York
In December dusks
When hats point to sea

55TH CHORUS

This means
   that everything
      has some home
     to come to
Light has windows
   balconies of iron
      like New Orleans

It also has all space
   And I have windows
      balconies of iron
        like New Orleans

I also have all space

And St Louis too

   Light follows rivers
     I do too

   Light fades, I pass

56TH CHORUS

Light illuminates
   The intense cough
Of young girls in love
Hurrying to sell their
      future husband
On the Market St
      Parade

Light makes his face
      reddern
   Her white mask

She sucks to bone him dry
   And make him happy
   Make him cry
      Make him baby
   Stay by me.

57TH CHORUS

Crooks of Montreal
     Tossing up their lighters
       To a cigarette of snow
       Intending to plot evil
       And break the pool machine
         Tonight off Toohey's head
         And the Frisco fire team
         Come howling round
         The corner of the dream

58TH CHORUS

Immense the rivets
In the broadsides
Of battleships
   Fired upon head on
   In face to face combat
   In the Philippines
      Anchored Alameda
      Overtime for toilets
        On Labor Day

59TH CHORUS

IL
 W
 U
  Has tough white seamen
  Scrapping snow white hats
  In favor of iron clubs
  To wave in inky newsreels
  When Frisco was a drizzle
      And Curran all sincere,
        Bryson just a baby,
 Reuther bloodied up,
 —When publications
Of Union pamphleteers
  Featured human rock jaws
  Jutting Editorialese
  Composed by angry funny
      redhead editors
 Walking with their heads down
   To catch the evening fleet
     And wave goodbye to sailors
       passing rosely dreams
     Into a sparkling cannon
       Gray & spiced & span
         To shine the Admiral
           In his South Pacific pan—

60TH CHORUS

No such luck
  For Potter McMuck
Who broke his fist
On angry mitts
In fist fights
Falling everywhere
From down Commercial
  To odd or even
All the piers
  Blang! Bang!
  I L W U had a hard time
  And so did N A M
  And S P A M
  And as did A M

61ST CHORUS

YOU INULT ME EVERY NIME, MALN BWANO
Ladies and Gentle-man
   The phoney woiker
  You here see
     Got can one time
  In Toonisfreu
     Ger ma nyeee
     Becau he had
        no dime
To give the con duck teur
     Yo see he stiffled
     For his miffle
And couldnt cough a little
     Bill de juice ran
       down his Sfam.

62ND CHORUS

JULIEN LOVE'S SOUND
"All
    right!
Here we are
  with all the little lambs.
Has anyone disposed
  of my old man
Last night?
    Mortuary deeds,
    Dead,
  Drink, me down
  Table or two,
  Wher'd you put it
    Kerouac?
  The bottoms in your bag
Of cellar heaven doors
And hellish consistencies
  Gelatinous & composed
  Will bang & break
Apon the time clock
  Beat prow stone bong
  Boy
  Before I give YOU
  An idgit of the
    Kind Love Legend"

63RD CHORUS

JULIEN LOVE'S JUDGMENT
"Seriously boy
This San Francisco
     Blues of yours
Like shark fins
     the summer before
And was it Sarie
Sauter Finnegan
   Some gal before—
   It's a farce
     For funny you
               you know?
I don't think I'll buy it"

Slit in the ear
   By a bolo knife
Savannah Kid just nodded
At the beast that
   Hides.

   Secret
   Poetry
   Deceives
Simply

64TH CHORUS

California evening is like Mexico
The windows get golden oranges
The tattered awnings flap
Like dresses of old Perdido
   Great Peruvian Princesses
     In the form of Negro Whores
     Go parading down the sidewalk
Wearing earrings, sweet perfume
    Old Weazel Warret

    tradesmen
     sick of selling
     out their stores stand in
      the evening lineup
      before identifying cops
      they cannot understand
      in the clouds of can
      and iron moosing
      marshly morse
      of over head

65TH CHORUS

Daughters of Jerusalem
Prowling like angry felines
Statuesque & youthful
  From the well
  Embarrassed but implacable
  And watched by hungry worriers
    Filling out the whitewall
      Car with 1000 pounds
      Of "Annergy!
        That's what I got!
      An-nergy!"
      To burn up Popocatepetl's
        Torch of ecstasy.

The neons redly twangle
  Twinkle cute & clean
  Like Millbrae cherry
    Nipptious tostle
      Flowers tattled
      Petal for the joss stick
      Stuck in neon twaddles
      To advertise a bar
  —All over SanFranPisco
64   The better is the pain

66TH CHORUS

—"Switch to Calvert"
   Runs an arrow eating
      Bulb by bulb
      Across the bulbous
         Whisky bottle
And under the Calvert clock

   Tastes better! Everyone
         Tastes better
         All the time

And fieldhands
That aint got aznos
   But the same south Mexican
   Evening soft shoe
      walk
Slow in dusts of soft
in Ac to pan
Here in Frisco City
      American
   The same way walk
      To buy some vegetables

67TH CHORUS

For the bedsprings on the roof
   Not keep the rain on out
Or bombed out huts
   In dumpland—Blue
Workjacket, shino pants,
  It's like Mexico all violet
   At ruby rose & velvet
     Sun on down
       On down
   Sun on down
   Sundown

Red blood bon neon
   Bon runs   don   blon

By Barrett
     Wimpole
        Trackmeet

68TH CHORUS

And like Mexico the deep
Gigantic scorpic haze
Of shady curtain night
  Bein drawn on civilized
  And Fellaheen will howl
    Where the cows of mush
Rush to hide their sad
  Tan hides in the stonecrump
  Mumps bump top of hill
    Out Mission Way
    Holy Cows of Cross
    And Lick Monastery

      Velvet for our meat
      Hamburgers

And doom of pained nuns
  Or painted
    One
  Mexico is like Universe

69TH CHORUS

And Third Street a Sun
Showing just how's done
The light the life the action
The limp of worried reachers
Crawling up the Cuba street
In almost dark
To find the soften bell
Creaming Meek on corner
One by one, Tem, Tim,
Click, gra, rattapisp,
Ting, Tang—

Blink!   Off
Run!   Arrow!
Cut!   Winkle!   Twinkle!
Fill
Piss!   Pot!
The lights of coldmilk
supper hill streets
make me davenport
and cancel Ship.

70TH CHORUS

3rd St is like Moody St
Lowell Massachusetts
It has Bagdad blue
  Dusk down sky
  And hills with lights
 And pale the hazel
       Gentle blue in the
            burned windows
Of wooden tenements,
  And lights of bars,
      music brawl,
"Hoap!" "Hap!" & "Hi"
In the street of blood
And bells billygoating
  Boom by at the ache
      of day
The break of personalities
  Crossing just once
  In the wrong door

71ST CHORUS

Nevermore to remain
  Nevermore to return
  —The same hot hungry
    harried hotel
  wild Charlies dozzling
    to fold the
    Food papers in the
      mahogany talk
Of television reading room
Balls are walled
  and withered
  and long fergit.

Moody Lowell Third Street
  Sick & tired bedsprings
    Silhouettes of brownlace
      eve night dowse—
All that—
  And outsida town
    The aching snake
  Pronging underground
    To come eat up
    Us the innocent
      And insincere in here

72ND CHORUS

And Budapest Counts
Driving lonely mtn. cars
On the hem of the grade
Of the lip curve hill
Where Rockly meets
  Out Market & More—
  The last shore—
    View of the sea
      Seal

Only Lowell has for sea
The imitative Merrimac

  And Frisco has for
        snake
      The crowdy earthquake
        cataract
And Hydrogen Bombs
      of Hope
  Lost in the blue
      Pacific
    Empty sea

73RD CHORUS

Bakeries gladly bright
Filled with dour girls
Buying golden pies
For sullen brooding boys

On 3rd St in the night

But by day
   The Greek Armenian
     Milk of honey
   Bee baclava maker
   Puts his sugars
   On the counter
     For bums with avid jaws
   And hollow eyes
     Eager to eat
     Their last dainty.

74TH CHORUS

Marchesa Casati
Is a living doll
Pinned on my Frisco
Skid row wall

Her eyes are vast
Her skin is shiny
Blue veins
And wild red hair
Shoulders sweet & tiny

Love her
Love her
    Sings the sea
  Bluely
 Moaning
In the Augustus John
    de John
      back ground.

75TH CHORUS

Her eyes are living dangers
'll Leap you
  From a page
Wearing the same insanity
  The sweet unconcernedly
  Italian humanity
    Glaring from black eyebrows
      To ask
      Of Renaissance:
    "What have you done now
    After 3 hundred years
    But create the glary witness
    Which out this window
    Shows a pale green
      Friscan hill
      The last green hill
      Of America
        With a cut   a band

76TH CHORUS

Of brown red road
  Coint round
  By architects of hiways
   To show the view
    To ledge travellers
Of Frisco, City, Bay
  And Sea
     As all you do is drive around
    —By Groves of lonesome
     Redwood trees
     Isolated
     In physical isolation
     On the bare lump
     Hill like people
      Of this country
     Who walk alone
      In streets all day
       Forbidden
       To contact physically
        Anybody
       So desirable—

77TH CHORUS

They kill'd all painters
Drown'd—Made wash
The smothering crone
Of Cathay,
  Flower of Malaya,
  And Dharma saws,
  Gat it all in,
    Like wash,
    Call'd it Renascence
    And then wearied
      From the globe—
        Hill, last hill
        Of Western World
          Is cut around
          Like half attempted
          Half castrated
          Protrudient breast
          Of milk
        From wild staring earth

78TH CHORUS

—The last scar
America was able
   To crate
   The uttermost hill
   Beyond which is just
         Pacific
   And no more sc-cuts
   And Alamos neither
   But that can be rolled
   In satisfying sea
   Absolved of suicide—
      Except that now
      They're blasting fishermen
        Apart?"

79TH CHORUS

"Beyond that fruitless sea"
—So speaks Marchesa
Mourning the Renaissance
And still the breeze
Is sweet & soft
   And cool as breasts
   And wild as sweet dark eyes.

Sits in her spirit
Like she wont be long
And bright about it
   All the time, like short
     star

     An angry proud beauty
     Of Italy

80TH CHORUS

San Francisco Blues
Written in a rocking chair
In the Cameo Hotel
San Francisco Skid row
Nineteen Fifty Four.

This pretty white city
On the other side of the country
Will no longer be
Available to me
I saw heaven move
Said "This is the End"
Because I was tired
of all that portend.

And any time you need
    me
Call
I'll be at the other
end
Waiting
    at the final hall

A NOTE ON SOURCES

Book of Blues, which includes "San Francisco Blues," "Richmond Hill Blues," "Bowery Blues," "MacDougal Street Blues," "Desolation Blues," "Orizaba 210 Blues," "Orlanda Blues," and "Cerrada Medellin Blues," is one of the unpublished manuscripts Jack Kerouac left in his meticulously organized archive. It does not contain all of Kerouac's unpublished blues poems—he chose not to include, for instance, "Berkeley Blues," "Brooklyn Bridge Blues," "Tangier Blues," "Washington DC Blues," and "Earthquake Blues." Comparisons with Kerouac's original handwritten notebooks indicate that in the process of editing the book, he deleted and rearranged some verses, and made some small editorial changes. Readers familiar with the excerpts from "San Francisco Blues," published in *Scattered Poems* (City Lights Books, 1971), will notice that he made changes in those verses.

—John Sampas, Literary Executor,
Estate of Jack and Stella Kerouac

PENGUIN 60s

are published on the occasion of Penguin's 60th anniversary

LOUISA MAY ALCOTT · *An Old-Fashioned Thanksgiving and Other Stories*

HANS CHRISTIAN ANDERSEN · *The Emperor's New Clothes*

J. M. BARRIE · *Peter Pan in Kensington Gardens*

WILLIAM BLAKE · *Songs of Innocence and Experience*

GEOFFREY CHAUCER · *The Wife of Bath and Other Canterbury Tales*

ANTON CHEKHOV · *The Black Monk* and *Peasants*

SAMUEL TAYLOR COLERIDGE · *The Rime of the Ancient Mariner*

COLETTE · *Gigi*

JOSEPH CONRAD · *Youth*

ROALD DAHL · *Lamb to the Slaughter and Other Stories*

ROBERTSON DAVIES · *A Gathering of Ghost Stories*

FYODOR DOSTOYEVSKY · *The Grand Inquisitor*

SIR ARTHUR CONAN DOYLE · *The Man with the Twisted Lip* and *The Adventure of the Devil's Foot*

RALPH WALDO EMERSON · *Nature*

OMER ENGLEBERT (TRANS.) · *The Lives of the Saints*

FANNIE FARMER · *The Original 1896 Boston Cooking-School Cook Book*

EDWARD FITZGERALD (TRANS.) · *The Rubáiyát of Omar Khayyám*

ROBERT FROST · *The Road Not Taken and Other Early Poems*

GABRIEL GARCÍA MÁRQUEZ · *Bon Voyage, Mr President and Other Stories*

NIKOLAI GOGOL · *The Overcoat* and *The Nose*

GRAHAM GREENE · *Under the Garden*

JACOB AND WILHELM GRIMM · *Grimm's Fairy Tales*

NATHANIEL HAWTHORNE · *Young Goodman Brown and Other Stories*

O. HENRY · *The Gift of the Magi and Other Stories*

WASHINGTON IRVING · *Rip Van Winkle* and *The Legend of Sleepy Hollow*

HENRY JAMES · *Daisy Miller*

V. S. VERNON JONES (TRANS.) · *Aesop's Fables*

JAMES JOYCE · *The Dead*

GARRISON KEILLOR · *Truckstop and Other Lake Wobegon Stories*

FOR THE BEST IN PAPERBACKS, LOOK FOR THE

In every corner of the world, on every subject under the sun, Penguin represents quality and variety—the very best in publishing today.

For complete information about books available from Penguin—including Puffins, Penguin Classics, and Arkana—and how to order them, write to us at the appropriate address below. Please note that for copyright reasons the selection of books varies from country to country.

In the United States: Please write to *Consumer Sales, Penguin USA, P.O. Box 999, Dept. 17109, Bergenfield, New Jersey 07621-0120.* VISA and MasterCard holders call 1-800-253-6476 to order all Penguin titles.

In Canada: Please write to *Penguin Books Canada Ltd, 10 Alcorn Avenue, Suite 300, Toronto, Ontario M4V 3B2.*

In the United Kingdom: Please write to *Dept. JC, Penguin Books Ltd, FREEPOST, West Drayton, Middlesex UB7 0BR.*